For Matthew
—R.L.U.

For Maira & Dastan
—Yusup

Petunia the Unicorn Moves to the Big City
Copyright © 2022 by Waystation Media LLC

Published by But That's Another Story... Press
Ridgefield, CT

Printed in the United States of America.

First Printing, 2022.
ISBN: 978-1-953713-17-9
Library of Congress Control Number: 2021925405

Petunia the Unicorn

Moves to the Big City

A Petunia Cupcake Fluffybottom Book

Written by R.L. Ullman
Illustrations by Yusup Mediyan

But That's
Another Story...
Press

Hello, my name is Petunia Cupcake Fluffybottom, but you can just call me Petunia. I'm a unicorn!

My family is a little different from other families. I live with my fabulous Auntie Sprinkles, my scrappy dog Gumdrop, and our loyal butler Winston.

We used to live in a land far, far away but we've just moved to Manhattan! Auntie Sprinkles purchased a beautiful brownstone on West 81st Street.

I've never lived in the human world before and I'm excited to experience everything it has to offer!

I love my Auntie Sprinkles. Her full name is Lady Rainbow Sprinkles Fluffybottom, but I call her Auntie Sprinkles for short. She's very giving, very gracious, and very, very glamourous.

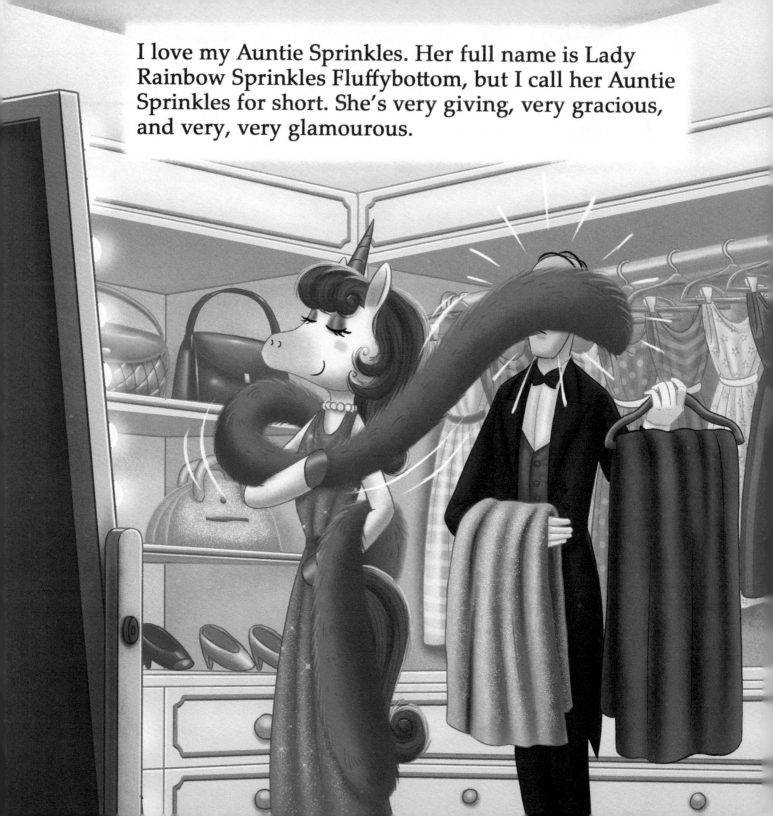

She's also quite the business tycoon.

Gumdrop is my cuddly companion. He might be small, but he's really brave. Well, most of the time anyway.

KRAKOOM!

Winston is the best. He doesn't say much, but he does most of the heavy lifting around here.

I'm excited to see all of the city's attractions, but wherever we go it seems like the biggest attraction is us! Like when we visited the Statue of Liberty…

And the Central Park Zoo...

Even Radio City Music Hall!

"Auntie Sprinkles, we seem to be the only unicorns in town," I say. "Do you think we'll like it here?"

"Of course, my love," she says, "Just like a rainbow's beauty comes from all of its different colors shining together, the city's beauty comes from all of its different people living together, and now that includes two terrific unicorns. Besides, I'd be surprised if anyone even noticed us."

"All the News That's Fit to Print"

The Manhattan Gazette

LATE CITY EDITION
Weather: Rain, warm today; clear tonight. Sunny, pleasant tomorrow. Temp. range: today 66-66; Sunday 71-66. Temp.-Hum. Index yesterday 68. Complete U.S. report on P. 53.

VOL. CXVIII. No. 50521

© 1969 The New York Times Company

NEW YORK, MONDAY

X

10 CENTS

Unicorns on West 81st Street!

Get ready to believe the unbelievable because unicorns have been spotted on West 81st Street! That's right, two real-life unicorns were seen enjoying a relaxing afternoon stroll with a rather feisty corgi along one of the most exclusive streets in Manhattan. It seems the unicorns have moved permanently to West 81st Street, shocking many of their new neighbors.

"Is this really happening?" asked Mrs. Harriett O'Dell, a long-time resident of West 81st Street. "I didn't even know unicorns were real!"

"I find this quite upsetting," said Mr. James Snobson, another resident. "No one notified me about this."

By the next morning, it seems like lots of people have noticed us.

After breakfast, Winston, Gumdrop, and I make our way through the crowd to deliver gifts to our new neighbors.

For some reason, they don't seem too happy to see us.

Especially the man next door. He tells us to keep our gift and slams the door shut.

SLAM!

Before we leave, I stop Gumdrop from leaving a gift of his own!

That afternoon, there's a loud knock, and to my surprise, it's that rude man from next door!

KNOCK!

KNOCK!

KNOCK!

"Good evening," he says coldly. "I am Mr. Snobson, your neighbor."

"Oh, Mr. Snobson, what a pleasure," Auntie Sprinkles says. "Please join us for a slice of Winston's divine Chocolate Chocolate Bundt Cake."

"I am not here for Chocolate Chocolate Bundt Cake," Mr. Snobson says, his face flush with anger. "I am here on behalf of the West 81st Street residents to complain about how you are ruining our street."

"Before you arrived everything was peaceful," Mr. Snobson says. "But now there are noisy crowds outside my door day and night. Unicorns do not belong in the human world, and they certainly do not belong on West 81st Street. I suggest you leave at once or I will ask the Department of Animal Control to throw you out!"

Then, he takes the slice of Winston's divine Chocolate Chocolate Bundt Cake and leaves.

"Auntie Sprinkles, what will we do?" I ask.

"Why, we're going to throw a dinner party, of course," she says.

"A dinner party?" I say confused.

"Yes, dear, a dinner party," she says. "Once our neighbors get to know us better everything will be just fine."

But I wasn't so sure. After all, if the neighbors didn't want us here then why would they come to our dinner party?

But Auntie Sprinkles had a solution for that.

What:
Dinner Party of the Century.

Where:
The Residence of Lady Rainbow Sprinkles Fluffybottom
at West 81st Street.

When:
Tomorrow 7:00 pm Sharp.

Dress:
Festive (bring your dancing shoes).

PS: Dinner will be followed by an extravagant
rooftop surprise.

Auntie Sprinkles is a whirlwind all day. She picks out an elegant outfit.

Creates a traditional unicorn dinner menu.

And selects hoof-tapping dance music.

I ask her what the 'extravagant rooftop surprise' is, but she won't tell me.
"That's why it's called a surprise, darling," is all she says.

Shortly after 7 o'clock the party is in full swing. Everyone in the neighborhood has arrived, except for one person.

Then, there's a knock at the door. It's Mr. Snobson! He came, but he doesn't look happy about it. After that, things fall apart fast.

Our traditional unicorn dinner is a disaster.

And no one joins us on the dance floor for the hoof-tapping music.

"This is the most dreadful dinner party I have ever attended," I hear Mr. Snobson say. "These unicorns clearly do not belong here."

Just then, Auntie Sprinkles rings a bell to get everyone's attention.

"Good evening ladies and gentlemen. The time has come for our extravagant surprise. Please join me on the rooftop deck."

I don't know what she has planned, but I sure hope it fixes this mess.

The rooftop is buzzing with curious excitement.

But then I hear Winston whisper in Auntie Sprinkles ear.

"I have bad news, Madam. The fireworks company just cancelled."

Auntie Sprinkles looks crushed.

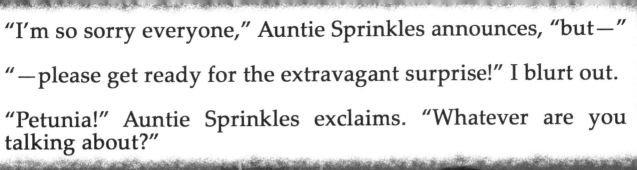

"I'm so sorry everyone," Auntie Sprinkles announces, "but—"

"—please get ready for the extravagant surprise!" I blurt out.

"Petunia!" Auntie Sprinkles exclaims. "Whatever are you talking about?"

"This!" I say. And then I concentrate hard.

"I-I've never seen a rainbow at night before," Mr. Snobson says. "It's beautiful. H-How did you do that?"

"Unicorn magic," I say proudly. "A rainbow isn't beautiful because it has lots of colors, it's beautiful because all of those colors shine together. We're all different, Mr. Snobson, but it's only when we bring those differences together that the world truly shines. Just like having unicorns on West 81st Street."

"I-I never thought about it that way." Mr. Snobson says. "I'm so sorry I asked you to leave. Would you please forgive me?"

"Of course," I say. "Would you like to come over tomorrow night? I'd be happy to make another rainbow."

"That sounds lovely," he says humbly. "Will you also be serving Winston's divine Chocolate Chocolate Bundt Cake?"

"Why, yes," Auntie Sprinkles says warmly. "I think we can arrange that."

And the next night was a wonderful night on West 81st Street.

R.L. Ullman is the bestselling author of award-winning books for kids. He creates fun, engaging characters that kids (and adults) want to read about. R.L. lives with his wife, son, two dogs, and a laptop in Connecticut. Find out what R.L. is up to at rlullman.com.

Yusup Mediyan is a freelance illustrator and animator who lives in West Java, Indonesia. He has illustrated children's books, book covers, and several animated series. He is also a father of two.

⭐⭐⭐⭐⭐

Reviews are important to bring this book to the attention of more readers. So, if you enjoyed this book, we would be very grateful if you could leave an honest review online. Thanks for your support! .

CPSIA information can be obtained
at www.ICGtesting.com
Printed in the USA
LVHW072255190322
713897LV00004B/78